Snow Scene

Richard Jackson

Pictures by
Laura Vaccaro Seeger

A NEAL PORTER BOOK
ROARING BROOK PRESS
NEW YORK

What are these?

Trees.

And those?

Shadows.

Icy bough.

Look here!

Red ear.

And there?

Frosty
hair.

What then?

Snowmen.

And since?

Small prints.

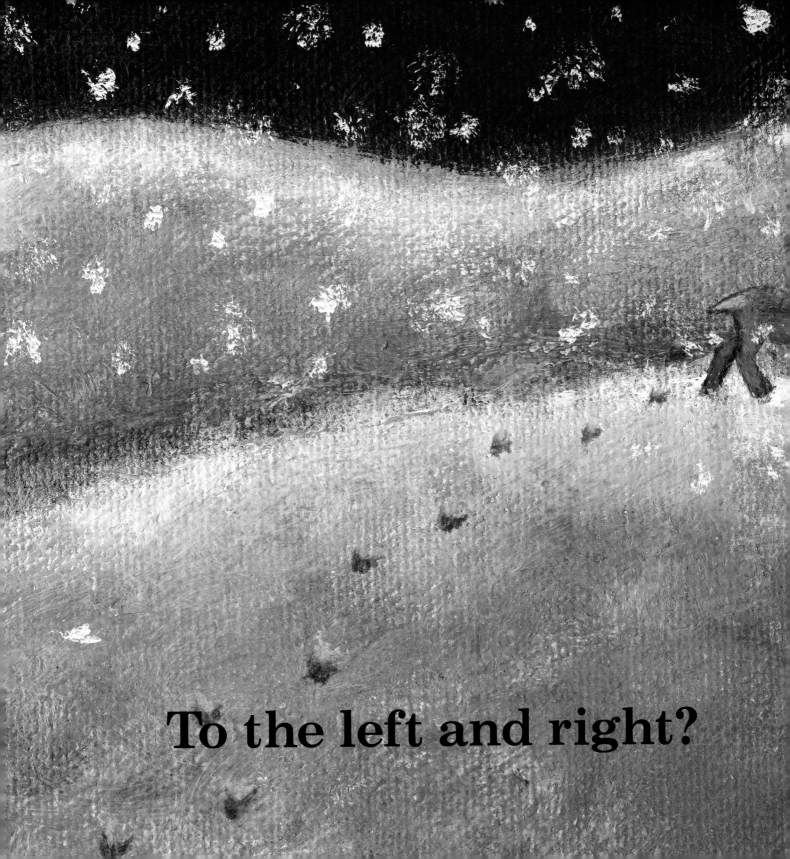

To the left and right?

Slight white.

Night white.

Quite light.

Bright light.

Just seen?

A hint of green.

And soon?

It's April . . .

May . . .

And then it's June.

Come, see this.

And this.

And this.

And will you
look at that?

Winter's hat!

For Neal Porter
Himself
—R.J.

For Jennifer Browne, with love and appreciation
—L.V.S.

Text copyright © 2017 by Richard Jackson
Illustrations copyright © 2017 by Laura Vaccaro Seeger
A Neal Porter Book
Published by Roaring Brook Press
Roaring Brook Press is a division of Holtzbrinck Publishing Holdings Limited Partnership
175 Fifth Avenue, New York, New York 10010
The artwork for this book was created using acrylic paint on canvas.
mackids.com

Library of Congress Cataloging-in-Publication Data

Names: Jackson, Richard, 1935– author. | Seeger, Laura Vaccaro, illustrator.
Title: Snow scene / Richard Jackson ; illustrated by Laura Vaccaro Seeger.
Description: First edition. | New York : Roaring Brook Press, 2017. | "A Neal
    Porter book." | Summary: "A playful guessing game set in a snowy
    landscape"— Provided by publisher.
Identifiers: LCCN 2016047531 | ISBN 9781626726802 (hardcover)
Subjects: | CYAC: Stories in rhyme. | Snow—Fiction. | Picture puzzles.
Classification: LCC PZ8.3.J1357 Sn 2018 | DDC [E]—dc23
LC record available at https://lccn.loc.gov/2016047531

Our books may be purchased in bulk for promotional, educational, or business use. Please
contact your local bookseller or the Macmillan Corporate and Premium Sales Department
at (800) 221-7945 ext. 5442 or by e-mail at MacmillanSpecialMarkets@macmillan.com.

First edition 2017
Printed in China by RR Donnelley Asia Printing Solutions Ltd., Dongguan City, Guangdong Province
1 3 5 7 9 10 8 6 4 2